DARK DESIGNS

R.S. PENNEY

DARK DESIGNS

The sun shone brightly in the clear blue sky, casting rays of silver light down upon the tops of pine trees that swayed in the wind. A line of them stood like vigilant sentinels, spreading shade across the green field.

Jena Morane watched them with fascination.

Behind her, a curving city street flowed like a river around houses that were hidden behind their own foliage. Through contact with her Nassai, she could feel people walking along the sidewalk. A pair of teenage girls if their silhouettes were any indication. The Holy Companion himself could not have made a more picturesque setting.

Dressed in black pants and a matching t-shirt, Jena stood with hands clasped behind her back. "How long am I going to have to stay here?" she asked of the man approaching from her left.

"You don't like it?"

Jena pursed her lips, turning her face up to the sky. She blinked when sunlight hit her eyes. "To be honest, I don't," she muttered. "There's something a little too perfect about Belos."

The man wore white pants and a black t-shirt, keeping his

eyes downcast as he approached. "Jena, Jena, Jena," he said, shaking his head. "You know what our friends from Earth would call this?"

"I suspect you'll tell me."

"They have a beautiful little phrase," Nate Calarin said. "They call it Digging up the Garden of Eden."

Chewing on her lip, Jena winced. She let her head hang, strands of short auburn hair falling over her face. "I'm not familiar with the reference," she said. "But I figure it has something to do with admonishing cynics."

Tall and slim, Nate stood with his arms folded, a smile on his dark-skinned face. "I would think you'd welcome an easy assignment," he said. "You've more than done your fair share of the difficult work."

"Then you don't know me," she snapped. "I've been here three damn months, Nate. Three. You know what my days consist of? Meet with the City Watch; check reports on crime. Scan sensor data for any ships passing through the system. Read the local news. Did you know they're erecting a monument to celebrate the tenth anniversary of this colony next week? Now you do."

Nate flashed a tiny smile, bowing his head to her. He chuckled softly, which only spiked her ire. "You are a tough one to please, Jena," he said. "Most Keepers would be pleased to have-"

"An assignment like this..."

Mouth hanging open, Jena threw her head back. She let out a frustrated groan. "I grew up on the Fringe, Nate," she grumbled. "Alaros. You know what it's like out there? Your summers are spent in a deluge."

"I fail to see-"

"The planet is really only habitable near its equator, and most of that is swamp. It's hard to eek out a life."

"There are other options, you know." Nate lifted his chin to stare at her with eyes that smoldered. "Your people could return to Leyria."

"But we like the challenge."

That was something that Core Worlders like Nate Calarin would never understand: the human need to push yourself to your limits. Leyria had designed solutions to provide for just about every human need – and the existence of such solutions was a good thing in her mind; no one should be forced to live without the basic necessities of survival – but some people chose to strike out on their own.

She turned around and found herself staring across the field to where the narrow road marked the edge of the residential sector. In the distance, the skyscrapers of the inner city glittered in the sunlight.

Jena frowned, nodding to herself. "Come on then," she said, hanging her head. She brushed hair away from her face. "We should get down to the Hub so I can go about my riveting daily routine."

THE HUB WAS a dome-shaped building at the centre of the city. On its top floor, a concourse of small stores formed a ring around open cafés. Tall trees in the central garden reached up toward the skylight.

Jena's office was on the second level of the concourse. Four cream-coloured walls surrounded a wooden desk with a single glass panel situated in the middle, and blinds on the window segmented the sunlight.

Jena breathed out a sigh.

One good thing about life as a Justice Keeper was that it offered you a fair amount of variety. She could set her own hours, prioritize her own agenda...and that would have been wonderful if there was some actual *work* for her to do. No one came to Belos! Most of the time, she was the only Keeper on this planet.

There simply wasn't much of a demand for one. The colony was little more than a few cities spread out on the coastline of the north-eastern continent. Perhaps two hundred thousand humans lived here. The presence of flora and fauna identical to that found on Leyria suggested this world had been modified by the Overseers to support a human colony, but if humans had ever lived here before Leyrian colonization, no sign of them remained. With such a low population, any black-market presence was minimal, and anything that did crop up could be handled by local security.

The glass panel on her desk was aligned vertically to serve as a computer access terminal. She tapped it and watched its clear surface burst alight with an array of icons on a field of green.

Jena closed her eyes, leaning her head against the cushion of her seat. She took a deep breath. "Another day in the biz," she said, nodding. "What's in the report this time? Maybe some jaywalking!"

She tapped an icon to bring up the local sheriff's report. Black text scrolled across a field of white with mug shots next to each description. Jena skimmed through them with half-hearted interest.

Touching the screen with splayed fingers, she flung the window aside to leave the app running. Her desktop reappeared. Space telemetry might be more interesting. She checked the results.

Seven ships had passed through the Belos system in the last five days, most only staying long enough to drop off supplies. One passenger liner had brought tourists along with a few immigrants and...

What was that?

Pursing her lips, Jena narrowed her eyes. "That can't be

right," she said, shaking her head. "Where in Bleakness did that come from?"

Long-range telemetry revealed a ripple in SlipSpace about a dozen light-years from here. Usually, the only thing that caused something like that was a passing ship, but this was much fainter than the kind of disturbance caused by a ship at high warp. *Something interesting, perhaps.*

She brought up the communications app, which displayed her contacts in a neat little list. Scrolling through, she found the man she was looking for. Double-tapping his name started the call.

A moment later, her screen was dominated by the pudgy face of a man with a ring of silver hair around the back of his skull. "Operative Morane," he said, squinting at her. "I guess you found something *else* to quiz me about."

Jena flashed a smile, a burst of heat in her face. She stared down into her lap. "Oh, you know me, Mort," she said, eyebrows rising. "Always looking for something to keep myself occupied."

"Indeed."

She forwarded the telemetry scans to his user account. "What could cause this kind of energy spike?"

Mort frowned, his face scrunched up as he read through the results. "I might say a ship," he muttered, leaning in close as if he was trying to get a better look. "Star-ships at high warp create a kind of ripple through SlipSpace that travels many times faster than the Speed of Light. That's how we can track them."

"Uh huh."

"But this is faint." Mort clasped his chin, nodding to himself. "My guess is it's nothing of consequence. There is a background radiation that permeates SlipSpace."

Crossing her arms with a grunt, Jena frowned down at herself. "Oh, sure," she said with a shrug. "Background radiation that just happens to spike in exactly the same place over the last three days."

Mort studied her with a frustrated expression, his beady eyes forced into a squint. "Sometimes high-energy leptons tunnel through SlipSpace," he said. "That could cause readings like this."

Pressing her lips together, Jena looked up at the man. She blinked several times. "Leptons," she said. "You really think a couple of sub-atomic particles could give off that much of an energy whammy?"

"They would have to be travelling close to the speed of light for us to detect them at this distance." Mort heaved out a sigh, bowing his head to stare at something on his desk. "But it's possible."

"How likely?"

"Operative Morane-"

"*How* likely?"

The man scratched his chin, wincing as though the simple act of considering the question brought pain. "I don't know," he admitted. "Not very. But we *have* seen periodic spikes in the radiation that permeates SlipSpace."

"Good enough." By pinching her fingers over the glass, Jena shrank the window that displayed Mort's image and deposited it in the lower left-hand corner of the screen. She brought up a list of available shuttles. "I think it's time I took a look."

With a groan, Mort pressed the palm of his hand to his forehead. He hunched over in his chair. "If you insist." The frustration in his voice was thick enough to stop a bullet. "But you won't find anything."

"I'll be the judge of that."

. . .

THE COCKPIT of the small assault-shuttle was illuminated by light that streamed in through the sloping canopy window, silver rays illuminating a large chair that had been positioned in front of a console. Through the pane, she saw the wall of the shuttle bay. Lights were flashing, indicating a launch in progress.

Jena approached the console.

Chewing on her lower lip, she winced and shook her head. "So, I'm flying off on a wild goose chase, huh?" she said, dropping into the pilot's chair. "We'll see what you all think when I bring back a golden egg."

Her fingers danced across the console, causing the touch-screen interface to burst alight with application windows. She powered the artificial gravity and activated the life-support systems.

Jena looked up through the window, blinking when the light hit her eyes. "This is Operative Morane, shuttle Larosa," she said into the comm unit. "I'm ready for take-off on your mark."

"Board is green, Operative Morane," a male voice answered. "Good luck."

She triggered the shuttle's VTOL system and watched as the concrete wall scrolled downward in her field of vision, the little craft rising into the air. A moment later, she was passing through the roof hatch.

Once through, she saw nothing but glittering buildings that stabbed the clear blue sky, sunlight glinting off every window. She angled the shuttle upward and keyed in a course for orbit.

Closing her eyes, Jena tilted her head back. She took a deep, soothing breath. "I'm on course for the upper atmosphere," she told the air traffic controller. "Everything looks good so far."

"Orbital traffic at a minimum," the voice replied. "You're clear."

She took off.

Now this was what she had signed up for! Nothing pleased Jena quite as much as a good mystery. Her parents had always told her she was really quite nosy, but if they couldn't understand the thrill of putting together all the puzzle pieces, then all she could do was feel sorry for them.

The strange readings had come from Neavos, a binary system roughly seventeen light-years away. At high warp, she would be there in a little under two hours. Plenty of time to catch up on her reading. She had forwarded the sheriff's report to the shuttle.

Mort was probably correct; in all likelihood, there was nothing interesting going on out there. At best, she would come back with some telemetry that made a few particle physicists quiver with excitement.

But it was worth a look.

Blue sky faded away, growing steadily darker as the stars appeared. Within a few minutes, the last wisps of the atmosphere were gone, and she had a clear view of the vast expanse of space.

"Setting course for Neavos," Jena said, tapping away at the console. "Tell Nate I'll see him at dinner."

"Roger that."

She powered up the warp drive and watched as the tiny points of light blurred into streaks that came together in the middle of the canopy window, creating a pulsing blob of radiance. That was what happened when you flew at superluminal speeds. Light seemed to compress into the distance in front of you.

Now the fun begins.

THE BLOB of light collapsed into a million tiny specs that spread out like dust hurled by a windstorm. Though nothing had changed, it felt almost as though a swarm of fireflies had surrounded the shuttle on all sides.

In the distance, Jena saw a bright spec of reddish light, which her instruments told her was a distant nebula. She brought up the console's communications menu, activating the SlipGate in the passenger compartment. That would allow her to communicate with her superiors on Belos in real time. "This is shuttle Larosa."

"Hello, Operative Morane," the male voice said. "I see you managed not to crash."

Jena grinned, her face suddenly aflame. She lowered her eyes to the console. "Well, I don't know who you've been talking to," she said, scooching closer. "But I'm one of the best pilots in the fleet."

"Oh really?"

"Mmmhmm."

She brought up a window on the touchscreen that displayed space telemetry. With a few tabs, she called up sensor data. "Everything looks normal," she said. "We have a very thin cloud of hydrogen, but-"

Jena blinked.

"Operative Morane?"

"Standby." Her instruments were telling her that she had stumbled upon a derelict ship some five thousand kilometres away. Could that have been what was causing the energy spikes? Beyond the limited range of a few light-seconds, ships were pretty much undetectable unless they went to warp. Perhaps this one was starting its engines. But that made very little sense. "Computer, place image on heads-up display."

The canopy window lit up with a wire-frame outline of the ship. Colour bled into the empty spaces, producing the image of a tube-like vessel that looked somewhat like the blade of a sword with a rounded tip.

Jena felt her jaw drop, blinking at the image. "No, that can't be..." She winced and gave her head a shake. "That's an old Wyvern-class troop carrier. Those haven't been in service for sixty years."

"You're sure?"

Gritting her teeth, Jena looked down into her lap. She tossed her head about with a grunt. "Believe me, I'm sure," she insisted. "That's Wyvern-class carrier alright. It must have drifted into the system."

She scanned the ship and found that several compartments along the dorsal hull had been exposed to the vacuum of space. The interior was intact. To her surprise, the ship responded to her probes by broadcasting the presence of active SlipGates.

"I think I've just received an invitation."

"Pardon?"

"The Gates report a nitrogen-oxygen atmosphere in the inner compartments." That would make sense if the crew had died before the life-support systems failed. "Internal temperature of...twenty-seven centigrade?"

That did *not* make sense.

Contrary to popular belief, ships did not freeze in space the instant their life-support systems failed. Quite the opposite, in fact. Sixty years of radiation build-up would make that place an oven. Unless the fins along the dorsal hull were doing their job of diffusing the heat. But why would they still be operational?

Tapping her lips with one finger, Jena closed her eyes. "I'm gonna take a look," she said, nodding to herself. "I don't know what's going on over there, but my gut tells me we don't want to find out the hard way."

"Alright. Be careful."

She swivelled around in her chair.

Slipping hands into her pockets, Jena stood and marched to the set of double doors at the back end of the cockpit. They slid open with a soft hiss, allowing her access to the passenger compartment.

A square table with four chairs was situated dead centre between four gray walls, and doors on both the port and starboard sides led to separate areas: one to a restroom, and the other to an airlock.

Behind the table, a large metal triangle stood silent and solemn with thin sinuous grooves along its surface. The Slip-Gate. Every shuttle had one, and they all served two functions. By the use of microscopic wormholes, they enabled FTL communication with any other Gate in the network. They also provided near instantaneous transit to any other Gate within a few hundred thousand kilometres.

Jena rounded the table.

Lifting her forearm, she studied the multi-tool that she wore on her gauntlet. She tapped away at the screen, interfacing with the Gate's systems. Two other Gates were in range, both on the ship. Safety protocols in their programming meant they wouldn't display as active if they weren't in suitable environments. Jena chose one.

A bubble of rippling energy closed around her body, making it seem as though the entire passenger compartment had been hidden behind a waterfall. Warped Space-Time. The Gate would send her and the air that surrounded her through SlipSpace.

She jerked forward.

For a brief instant, it seemed as though she were travelling down a dark, endless tunnel; then a new environment surrounded her. This one was equally dark. She couldn't see a damn thing. For half a second, she thought she was in space. Safety protocols or not, darkness was scary.

The bubble popped.

Lights came on, illuminating a large cargo bay with lots of open floor space. A few metal crates had been stacked against the wall, and a display screen listed their contents. Other than that, the room was empty.

Biting her lower lip, Jena tilted her head back. She blinked. "At least I can breathe in here," she said, stepping forward. "That's always a plus. Blood stains from exploding lungs are so last season."

She tapped away at her multi-tool, establishing a communications linkup with her shuttle. "You still there, Belos?" The shuttle would relay her words through the SlipGate, to her contacts back home. "I never got your name."

"I'm here," he replied. "My name is Vick."

A quick scan of the cargo manifest told her each crate's contents. There was nothing out of the ordinary: a few assault rifles, some medical supplies, engineering tools. Pretty much what you would expect on a military ship.

Craning her neck, Jena frowned up at the display screen. She squinted, shaking her head. "So far, I haven't seen anything special," she said. "Nothing that would explain an energy spike in SlipSpace at least."

She paced across the room.

The huge double doors opened automatically, revealing the gray wall of a hallway outside the cargo bay. Lights flickered on out there. The ship must have been following an energy conservation protocol.

Jena mopped sweat off her face, brushing a hand through her hair. "It's a little too hot in here," she muttered. "I'm starting to wonder if maybe the environmental controls are malfunctioning."

Once she passed through the door, she found herself in a long narrow corridor that curved slightly to her right. There was no sign of the crew. The place was devoid of life of any kind.

She used her multi-tool to scan for life-signs but found nothing. It was starting to occur to her that boarding the creepy derelict ship might not have been such a good idea, but Jena Morane was the sort of cat who maintained an on-again off-again relationship with curiosity. The urge to poke her nose in where it didn't belong would show up in the middle of the night and say, "No, baby, this time it'll be different, I swear." Though her better judgment would warn against it, she would always give in.

Something was nagging at her, but she couldn't quite put her finger on what it was. Despite the heat, she had to suppress the urge to shiver. Something about this ship was *wrong*. It almost felt like...like something was watching her.

Hair stood on the back of her neck.

Jena spun around, drawing her pistol from the holster on her belt. She raised it in both hands and found...nothing.

Just an empty hallway.

Jena let her head hang, wincing so hard sweat oozed from her pores. "Something's not right here," she said for her Nassai's benefit. The symbiont offered positive feelings in response. "Do you sense anything?"

No response.

Well, if her symbiont *had* sensed anything, it would have shared that knowledge with her. So it was a stupid question. "Operative Morane?" Vick's voice sounded from her multi-tool. "Were you talking to me?"

"No," she said. "My Nassai."

"Oh."

"Multi-tool active," she ordered, lifting her forearm. "Display layout for Wyvern-Class battle cruisers. Holographic readout."

A deck-by-deck map of the ship shimmered into existence in front of her, marking her position with a flashing red dot. If the blueprint was accurate, she wasn't far from the med-lab. That might be a good place to access ship logs.

Where were the bodies? If the ship had been damaged and set adrift in space, then what had become of its crew? It was a little macabre to realize that she would feel more comfortable in the presence of corpses than she would in this empty hallway, but corpses would make sense. An empty ship suggested that someone had been here and removed the bodies.

A left turn at the nearest intersection, a climb up to the next deck and a hard right brought her to the chief medical officer's office. The double doors slid open to reveal a small room with a kidney-shaped desk and a painting on the back wall. A window along the wall to her right looked in on the med-lab.

Jena stepped through the door with arms crossed, shaking her head. "I'll see if I can get a look at the logs," she told Vick. "Find out what happened to send this ship on a sixty-year death cruise."

Through the office window, she saw something down on the main floor of the med-lab. Stasis pods – perhaps a dozen of them. Each one was a tube just under three meters in length with a glass screen that looked in on the occupant.

She couldn't resist the urge to take a look.

The CMO's office was connected to the med-lab via a set of steps that went down to the lower level. "I think the crew might be in stasis," Jena told Vick. "I found pods in the medical bay."

"Do *not* revive them."

"Who has two thumbs and isn't an idiot?" she teased. "This girl."

Peering into the nearest pod, she found a man with pale features and stubble along his firm jawline. His eyes were closed, his dark hair brushed back. The tan uniform that he wore bore a patch on the upper arm. Red and white stripes with a square of blue in the upper left corner. She had seen that image before. It tickled her memory, but she couldn't place it no matter how she tried.

Jena pursed her lips as she stared into the pod. "Well, this is unnerving." She let her head hang, wiping sweat off her brow. "Whoever these people are, I don't think they are the original crew."

"What do you mean?"

Biting her underlip, Jena winced. She shook her head and let out a soft sigh. "They have markings that aren't Leyrian," she explained. "It looks to me like someone abducted them and brought them here."

"For what purpose?"

"I can't say."

Once again, she had the distinct impression that something was watching her. This time, however, she chose not to turn. Instead, she called on her Nassai and used spatial awareness to see the world around her. There was nothing in the room with her. Unless, of course, you counted the stasis pods.

The sensation seemed to be coming from the window. She turned and saw nothing there except the ceiling of the CMO's office. What was going on here? Was it just nerves or something more?

"Alright," she said. "I think we're done here. I'll access the logs and make my way back to the shuttle."

"Good idea."

TRYING to access the ship's logs proved to be a bust. She had spent nearly forty-five minutes at the CMO's work terminal, trying to find something useful. Every last morsel of information had been purged from the central computer. She couldn't even find any record of the ship's name.

The computer's operating system had been wiped, leaving the ship with only a few emergency functions that were largely handled by firmware. Life-support would remain active, but weapons, propulsion and communications were all offline. Even the security systems were down. Any door on this ship would open for anyone who happened to walk by without the need for an access code.

The SlipGates were still working, but those were separate systems – Overseer tech that her people had appropriated – and not under the direct control of the main computer. That left her with many questions.

Most stories were centred around six basic pieces of information: who, what, when, where, why and how. The one that interested Jena most was *why*. It irked her when she couldn't answer that question.

She knew this much: whatever had happened to this ship had been no accident. It took deliberate effort to set a ship adrift, to remove its crew, to kidnap humans from non-Leyrian colonies and hold them in stasis. At this point, her money was on pirates. Human trafficking was still an issue out on the Fringe. It would be hard for pirates to crack the access codes to a military ship, but not impossible. Perhaps those energy spikes that she had detected were small pirate vessels leaving the area. A skilled pilot could make a warp ripple appear to be background radiation. The process involved jumping to warp for mere milliseconds at a time before dropping back to sub-light velocity. It was a massive strain on your engines, but it would hide you from anything but the most intensive scan.

She made her way back to the cargo bay, glancing over her shoulder at least once every minute to make sure nothing was following her. All she ever saw was hallway. That did nothing to soothe her apprehension.

It's just nerves, Jena, she told herself. *Anyone would be creeped out by spending an hour on a derelict ship with people trapped in stasis pods.* A trained Keeper didn't jump to conclusions, didn't let fear get the better of her. There was a maxim among the people of Earth that she liked: don't add unnecessary complications to your theories. Piracy was the most likely explanation for all of this. No need to work herself into a lather imagining some invisible fiend stalking her.

She breathed a sigh of relief as she approached the cargo

bay doors. In a few hours, she would be back in her office receiving a commendation for her diligence. The Keepers would send a team to recover the ship. She strode into the cargo bay with a spring in her step. And they'd had nerve to say that she was grasping at-

The SlipGate was gone.

It had been right there by the back wall: a triangle identical to the one on her shuttle with grooves over its surface. Four hundred pounds of solid metal that would require an anti-gravitation unit to transport. That confirmed it.

Something was on this ship with her.

And now she was stuck here.

Jena licked her lips, then lowered her eyes to the floor. "Stay calm," she whispered to herself. "Belos Colony, can you hear me? This is Operative Jena Morane. Can you hear me, Belos Colony?"

No response.

Lifting her forearm, she tapped away at her multi-tool and felt a stab of terror when she realized she was no longer in contact with her shuttle. Her tool could not detect the Gate on board.

Jena slapped a hand over her face, raking fingers through her hair. "You can survive this," she said, blinking a few times. "Just think. If you can't use your own to call home...use the other one on this ship."

She performed a scan with her multi-tool and discovered there were no active SlipGates on this ship. Someone had depowered them. Ships usually only did that when they were about to go into battle to prevent enemy forces from Gating aboard during the conflict. "So where would they keep-"

The Deployment Room!

A common tactic in warfare was to use a shuttle to drop a Gate down on a planet's surface, then send troops through without the need for drop-ships. That was why most battle cruisers had two Gates onboard.

She turned and ran through the door.

Jena sprinted up the hallway, sweat slicking her face and matting dark hair to her brow. "Don't panic, Morane," she said, tossing her head about. "You've been in worse situations than this."

Intersections passed on her left as the hallway made a gentle curve inward toward the front of the ship. In the distance, lights turned on as sensors detected her presence and anticipated her destination. With any luck, whoever or whatever had moved the cargo bay Gate had not yet had a chance to move the second one. She could power it up with a few commands from her multi-tool.

She rounded a corner.

This corridor cut across the interior of the ship from starboard to port side, lights turning on at her approach. "At least the damn power conservation algorithms are still working! Always find the bright side, Jen!"

Clenching her teeth, Jena squeezed her eyes shut. She hissed air through them in a ragged breath. "Not much longer," she assured herself. "Use the Gate, send a distress call, then hold out until help arrives."

She had memorized the layout of the ship – enhanced spatial awareness was one of the many perks that came with a Nassai bond – and, therefore, she turned right at the next intersection, heading toward the bow of the ship.

The huge double doors were on her left. If the plans that she had looked up were accurate, those would lead to a large staging room that troops used before their missions. So far, she had felt no sign of whatever else was onboard.

She stepped through.

The room was indeed vast: a large cube of gray walls without one single feature to distinguish one from the other. By her estimate, a good three hundred people could easily share this space. She had made it, but there was no SlipGate here.

Its absence was not what made her heart try to burst out of her chest. A man stood in the middle of the floor. Tall and lean, he wore a tan uniform with a pistol on one hip and a stun baton on the other.

It took only a moment for her to recognize the man from the stasis tube. He stood before with eyes closed, perfectly serene. "Hello?" Jena called out. "Do you know where you are?"

His eyes snapped open.

Well...perhaps *eyes* was not the correct word. The material that filled his eye-sockets was a silvery metallic substance that reflected the lights overhead. He regarded her for a very long moment.

The man started forward. It was then Jena realized she had been herded here. This conflict had been ordained from the moment she had set foot on this ship. Possibly sooner. *Could he have lured me out here? Those energy spikes that caught my attention. Could it have all been a ploy?*

The man drew the pistol from its holster, raising the gun in one hand to point at her. He studied her with those gleaming metallic eyes. Dead eyes. Something else was at play here. The tissue on that man's body might still be alive, but there was no soul in his gaze. For all intents and purposes, he was dead.

Dropping to her knees, Jena raised hands up in front of herself. She concentrated, forming a bubble of rippling energy around her body. This was another benefit that came from bonding a Nassai. Time passed more quickly for her than it did for him, giving her a few moments to react.

To her eyes, the man was a blurry statue who stood with one arm extended, his gun pointed at a spot above her head.

CRAAAAAAAACK! The roar of a chemically propelled weapon filled the air.

A bullet emerged from his gun, spiralling toward her. She ignored it, focused instead on the tingling sensation in her body. She could only hold this Bending for a few seconds before the pain became too great.

Jena drew her own pistol, powering it on. She thrust her arm out to take aim, her finger wrapped around the trigger.

The bubble vanished.

She fired.

Bullets chewed through the man's body, causing some silver fluid to erupt from the wounds. He staggered backward without a single bit of emotion on his face, as though the gunshots had been mere annoyances.

With her mouth agape, Jena looked up at him. She blinked in confusion. "Alright, that's new," she said. "Don't suppose you might want to give up the sexy taciturn act and provide some exposition."

He aimed at her.

She threw her pistol and watched it tumble through the air to strike his hand just before he could get a fix on her. Both pistols went flying, and the man stared at his open palm as though surprised to find it empty.

The dead man pulled the stun baton from his belt, flinging it out to the side. Sparks flickered on the tip. If that thing touched her, it would provide a jolt strong enough to put even a Keeper down.

Jena stood.

The dead man paced around her in a circle, putting his back to the wall on her right. He stood there for a long moment, the sparking baton at his side. Not moving so much as an eyelash.

Jena pursed her lips, lifting her chin to stare down her nose at him. "Is it my move then?" she asked, raising an eyebrow.

"Well, alright, sweetheart. If you really want to be gracious, I'll go first."

She ran for him.

The man raised his baton up in a guarded stance, shielding his face with its flashing tip. He offered no expression, no sign of fear or rage or concern. What was this thing, and where had it come from? Was she in the presence of a literal killing machine?

He swung for her temple.

Jena crouched, bringing a hand up to strike his wrist. She punched him square in the chest with the other. The impact sent him stumbling backward.

The dead man pushed off the wall. He flung himself forward, and the next thing Jena saw was his knee colliding with her face. Her vision blurred as she fell over backward to land on her ass.

In her mind's eye, she saw the dead man fly over her and land several feet away with his back turned. He twirled the sparking stun-baton in his hand, preparing himself for round two.

Jena sprang off the floor.

She rounded on her opponent with fists raised in a guarded stance. "Okay, so it's good to know you've still got it." What exactly had animated a corpse wasn't something she wanted to think about.

The man spun around to face her, silver eyes staring at her from a face that was just too slack. He charged forward, the baton sparking in his hand, whistling with its electric whine. He tried to shove it in her face.

Jena turned sideways, evading the hit. She spun and brought her elbow around to connect with his cheek. The sudden *crunch* of shattered bone would have meant a knockout for any other opponent.

This one only stumbled away, raising a hand to steady his

balance. He made it all the way to the double doors on the far side of the room. *What in Bleakness is doing this? How is he standing?*

Her opponent threw the stun baton.

Crouching down, Jena raised both hands and erected a Bending that caused the air before her to ripple. The baton tumbled end over end across the room, coming to a stop just in front of her before rising up toward the ceiling.

The Bending vanished just in time for her to see the dead man coming toward her. He charged like a bull, then jumped and kicked her in the belly.

Jena went flying backward at heart-wrenching speed, colliding with the metal wall and dropping to the floor. "Damn it!" she hissed as she fell to her knees. "What kind of demon are you?"

Baring her teeth in a snarl, Jena winced. She felt hot tears roll over her cheeks. "I hate to tell you this, boyo," she said, getting to her feet. "But this girl has been fending off monsters since childhood."

He charged at her.

Jena jumped.

She did the splits in the air, allowing him to pass beneath her, then dropped to the floor. Bending over, she kicked out behind herself. The sharp hit to his spine flattened him against the wall.

Jena whirled around.

The dead man turned, staring at her with those metallic eyes. If he felt even a spec of pain, he didn't show it. What was this thing? She was beginning to feel all sorts of fear in her belly.

Jena threw a punch.

He ducked, letting the blow pass over his head. He delivered an uppercut to her chest that lifted her right off the ground. Pain slashed through her body as Jena sailed across the room.

She landed on her back. This thing shrugged off injuries. Beating the crap out of it wasn't going to do her any good. She had to find some other way to incapacitate her foe before he killed her.

Her multi-tool beeped.

The screen revealed something Jena would not have expected. Some kind of electromagnetic signal was emanating from the dead man. A carrier wave! Did that mean someone was controlling him remotely?

"Multi-tool active!" she bellowed. "White noise protocol!"

The man spasmed as though jolted by an electric current, his legs going out from under him. He dropped to his knees, then fell limply to the white-tiled floor, spread out on his belly.

Mopping a hand over her face, Jena pushed hair back from her eyes. "Well, I guess it could have been worse," she said, blinking. "I'm still breathing, and now I know how to kill you bastards."

The man began to rise.

Checking her multi-tool revealed that the signal emanating from his body had nearly doubled in intensity, more than enough to cut through her interference. Whoever was pulling this guy's strings was back in control.

The stun baton was lying on the floor a few feet away, still whistling with that high-pitched whine. She snatched it up in one hand, charging it to full power. "Alright, you son of a bitch," Jena hissed, standing up. "Game on."

He started toward her.

She charged at him with the baton in hand, its sparking tip flashing with every step. The man kept his steely gaze fixed on her, his arm stretched out to the side as if he meant to bash her skull in.

He swung at her ear.

Jena ducked.

She slipped past him on the right, then flung her arm out to strike the back of his neck with the baton. The man spasmed, his limbs flailing as he took a few stumbling steps and fell to the floor. Modifications or not, the body was still human. A shock like that would make it difficult to control his limbs.

Jena turned and ran. The pistol she had thrown was lying on the floor just a few feet away. She stopped long enough to scoop it up, returning it to its holster, and then made a break for the double doors.

They slid apart to let her run into the gray-walled corridor. Once outside, she felt another spike of panic. A tall man with dark skin and shaved head blocked her path. Just like the other, his eyes were silver.

She didn't need to look to sense the woman behind her – bonding with a Nassai let you perceive the world in all directions – but a quick glance revealed her to be a tiny slip of a girl in a denim skirt and tank top. Platinum blonde hair framed a pale face with the same metallic eyes.

Jena bared her teeth, a wince twisting her features. She shook her head with a growl of frustration. "That's just great!" The harshness in her voice surprised her. "Party never stops with you guys, huh?"

The man came at her.

He strode down the hallway with grim purpose, his expression blank as he moved on nimble feet. "Well then," Jena said. "At least I get a workout. Doc says I don't hit the gym nearly enough."

He tried to backhand.

Jena ducked and shoved the baton into his belly. Electric current caused the guy to spasm, his arms and legs shaking. She flicked the stick up to hit the underside of his chin, leaving a nasty burn.

Blondie came at her from behind, arms spread wide with

fingers curled as though she meant to claw furrows in skin. She jumped, wrapping her legs around Jena's waist, seizing Jena's head.

Jena bent over.

The woman's own momentum sent her flying upside-down over her fallen partner. She went all the way to the corner where two hallways met, then slammed into the wall and fell to the floor.

Face glistening, Jena chewed on her lower lip. She nodded once in approval. "And the bitch goes down," she said. "So that's Jena three, evil zombie pawns zero. Just in case you were keeping score."

She spun around and ran. At this point, her only hope was to get to the shuttle bay and pray that whatever had set up this little game hadn't had time to move or disable the shuttles. She absolutely hated feeling like a mouse in a maze. If she survived this, she was going to find the culprit and carve herself a pound of flesh.

People could not fight their fundamental nature, and Jena Morane was no exception to that rule. Even now, postulating hypotheses on *why* this had happened. Something had created its own little squadron of killing machines. So what purpose could it have in bringing her here?

The best way to answer that was to consider the process by which any other piece of technology was built. First there was the design phase, then the actual manufacturing and then...

Then quality control.

This was a test.

These creatures were immune to pain, capable of with-standing gunshots and they possessed a near endless supply of stamina. What better way to test their effectiveness than by pitting them against a hardened warrior. Keepers were famous for their skill in combat. If you want to prove the viability of a new product, throw it up against the best that the competition had to offer.

Blondie was chasing her down the corridor, no more than a few hundred feet away and running at a speed that might outpace a well-bred stallion. Jena didn't have to look to know that the woman would run her down in mere moments.

Worse yet, the two men weren't far behind. Apparently, they had recovered from the shocks she'd given them – so she could add healing factor to the list of advantages these creatures possessed – and now they wanted a little payback. Or whatever was controlling them did.

Jena did *not* possess infinite stamina. Her muscles were aching, her body driven to the point of exhaustion and she could feel the strain in her symbiont. If she didn't get her ass off this ship soon, they would kill her.

A man stepped out from a door in front of her.

Jena threw the baton.

It tumbled end over end through the air before striking him square in the forehead and flashing. Electric current pulsed through his body, causing him to flail about and fall to the floor.

Strange. He should have caught the baton. It had been pure instinct that made her throw it, and she had regretted it the instant the weapon left her fingertips. These things had remarkable reflexes. In a one-on-one fight, they were capable of holding their own against a Justice Keeper.

So why hadn't this one displayed some of those amazing reflexes? Could it be that controlling too many of these drones at the same time was taxing the puppet master to his cognitive limits? Advantage Jena.

She drew the pistol from her belt holster.

Spinning around, Jena raised the gun in one hand and narrowed her eyes. "EMP!" she shouted, watching as the LEDs on her pistol's barrel turned white. "I think you guys are in for a shocking good time."

She loved terrible puns.

Pulling the trigger, she sent an electrically charged slug into the chest of the blonde woman. Silver fluid exploded from the wound, and the woman thrashed about, falling to her knees.

Jena fired again. Blue tracers sped down the hallway, striking the dark man and his fair-skinned companion in turn. They both fell to the floor, overwhelmed by the current. EMP rounds were designed to overload the circuits of mechanized battle drones. They were Bleakness itself on the human nervous system.

She ran for it.

THE SHUTTLE BAY was two decks down and located near the bow of the ship. That was a problem since the zombie-things had forced her to run toward the stern. She had decided to use the ladders in maintenance shafts to climb down rather than ride in the elevators. It would be too easy to corner her that way.

Luck, it seemed, was on her side because she made it to the lower deck without any further altercations. That did very little to soothe her nerves. The intelligence controlling those creatures had been able to anticipate her every move so far. It had herded her like a cow to the slaughter.

With both SlipGates unavailable, the only way off this ship was a shuttle. Using an escape pod would almost certainly get her killed. They had no warp drive units, and that meant she would float helplessly in space while the enemy obliterated her with a few well-aimed particle beams. A shuttle was her only option.

Unless...

Closing her eyes, Jena tilted her head back. She took a deep breath and then let it out again. "Think," she said, nodding to herself. "Think before you act. Never give your enemy what he expects."

They wanted her to take a shuttle? Were there any other options? She had no doubt that these creatures meant to kill her; if she lived, it would mean she would spread the tale of what had happened here.

So what if she could convince them she was dead?

Jena frowned, staring down at the floor. She shook her head. "Risky," she muttered, starting up the corridor. "If they get so much as a whiff of what you're doing, it's down to the zombie town for you."

What did she know?

True, her enemies could scan for life signs just as she had when she came aboard, but that was by no means foolproof. Detecting crowds was easy; detecting individuals, not so much. After all, the only way a scanner could detect a human body was by its heat or electric field, and she was surrounded by things that were both hot and pulsing with electricity. You generally had to be in close proximity to get an accurate reading.

The ship did have motion sensors that tracked her movements, but with the central computer offline, her opponents would never be able to access that information – which meant she had some wiggle room.

Pressing a palm to her forehead, Jena winced. She raked her fingers through sweat-slick hair. "Okay," she said. "So taking an escape pod would be suicide, would it? Well, goodbye, cruel world."

SECURING the helmet over her head, Jena blinked through the large round visor. "There now," she said, lifting a gloved hand up in front of herself. She wiggled fingers. "I've always wanted to go for a space walk."

She stood in the middle of a supply room in a bulky steely gray space suit with a helmet the size of a fish bowl. "Easy now, Jen," she said, stepping forward. Maneuvering in this thing was a pain.

The double doors slid open, and she found herself in a narrow corridor with gray walls that ran toward the port side of the ship. What she wouldn't give to have someone turn off the artificial gravity. These suits were designed for weightlessness.

Jena closed her eyes, breathing deeply. "You can do this," she said, sweat beading on her brow, matting auburn hair to her skin. "You're just going for a little walk outside the ship. There's nothing to be afraid of."

Except that she might suffocate alone in the void.

At the end of the corridor, a round air-lock led to one of the ship's many emergency escape pods. Knowing her luck, silver-eyed fiends would come around the corner at any moment, and she would have to fight them in this bloody monstrosity of a suit.

She reached the air-lock.

Pressing a button on the wall, she opened the air doors and stepped into the small compartment beyond. The pod's hatch was open, allowing her to see inside. It was a dark tube with benches on each wall and a control panel at the far end.

Jena stepped inside.

Escape pods did not generate enough power to create an artificial gravity field, and she felt weightlessness kick in the instant she was through the hatch. That actually made things easier. She maneuvered to the control console.

Tapping away at the screen, she keyed in a launch and set a delay of one minute. The hatch would remain open until the last second to allow any other crew members who might have been straggling a chance to get onboard.

Jena shuffled back through the pod's interior. She was keenly aware of every single passing second. If she was on this thing when it launched, that was it. She was finished. With a sigh of relief, she stepped back into the air-lock.

Only then did she notice that the suit's bulky structure impaired her Nassai's ability to perceive what was going on behind her. Her symbiont could not see through walls, and apparently the suit was solid enough to block its spatial awareness. Odd. Ski masks posed no difficulty – she had worn one without any serious impairment to her 360-degree vision – but space suits were a problem. All the more reason to get off this ship.

The air-doors closed.

The pod's hatch slid shut as well, and it pushed away from the ship with a sudden jolt of motion. It sped off into the inky blackness, trailing thruster exhaust in its wake. With nothing to create a seal, the atmosphere that had filled the air-lock blew outward, pushing Jena into the void.

A small flash in the distance.

The pod had been destroyed. So it was true: her enemies had a ship lurking nearby to gun her down if she tried something like this. With any luck, they now thought she was dead. A single human in a space suit would be undetectable to their sensors. She was a cold object, giving off no radiation and there was plenty of *that* to be had out here.

Jena triggered her suit's thruster pack, using it to speed away from the ship as fast as she could manage. Acceleration made her stomach lurch, but she didn't care. She had to put some distance between herself and her adversaries.

The endless expanse of stars filled her vision: billions of tiny lights spread out in the blackness, all flickering and pulsing. They were much clearer than they would be on a planet's surface.

Now, what to do next?

She'd lost contact with her shuttle, she had twelve hours' worth of air and she was flying off into the deepness with nothing but a small pack of thruster fuel. The chances of anyone finding her were slim. She could command her multi-tool to broadcast a distress beacon, but that would make her visible to friend and foe alike. Faking her death would do no good if she spoiled it now.

These concerns had been in her mind while she formulated this plan. The fact was that trying to fly off in a shuttle would almost certainly result in her being shot down, and using an escape pod was even worse. She could only hope and pray that faking her death would convince her enemies to leave and that help would arrive before she ran out of air. A rescue ship *was* on its way. Her superiors would have dispatched one the instant they had lost contact with her. That was protocol.

Jena killed her thrusters.

By wrenching her arms and wiggling her hips several times, she was able to twist her body around for a view of the ship. It took several attempts, but she was able to spin around and face the direction she had come from.

She was now flying backwards, moving away from the ship that receded into the distance. She saw it mainly as a black gap in the field of stars – there was very little light out here – but she was now far enough to glimpse the whole thing from stem to stern. So far, no one had detected her.

So she floated, alone in the void. With the prospect of dying out here looming, she thought of all the people she would never see again. Ex-boyfriends, ex-girlfriends. Jena had never been good at settling down. Too independent. There were moments when she wondered if that had been a failing. She dismissed such thoughts quickly enough. Jena Morane had lived her life the way she wanted. Very few people could say the same.

A great deal of time – perhaps an hour, perhaps more –

passed while she watched the ship. She saw the occasional flicker of light that might have been a shuttle buzzing around the thing like a bee around a flower. Why would shuttles be-

The stasis pods.

Whoever was out there was collecting the stasis pods before departing. That left Jena with a queasy sensation in her belly. There were more of those...things, and who or whatever had engineered them could not possibly have good intentions.

Another fifteen minutes or so – by now the ship was so far off she could not even make out its silhouette against the blackness – and something happened. Points of light appeared like new stars being birthed.

They made streams of yellowish energy that came together like spokes on a wheel, charging a central emitter. Then a thick beam of light shot out of the darkness and struck something. The derelict ship. She saw its silhouette in the blast.

Most people would have expected a fireball; Jena knew better. There was a brief flare of ignited oxygen and then darkness. Explosions in space were lackluster things until you understood their true power. Shrapnel from the remains of that ship would be flying off in all directions, some of it coming her way.

Some of it might even overtake her.

That was not what left her feeling cold inside. Jena had seen that kind of weaponry before. Memories from her trip to Earth flashed in her mind. The Valiant had stopped to investigate a planet in Dead Space, searching for Anna Lenai.

With her mouth hanging open, Jena blinked. She winced and shook her head inside the helmet. "Overseers," she whispered. "Dear Companion, they're really out there! They *made* those monstrosities!"

There was a ripple in the distance that she recognized as the formation of a warp bubble. The Overseer ship had departed, having tied everything up in a neat little bow. With

Jena *dead* there would be no witnesses. Any rescue ship would assume she had died in the explosion and stop searching for her.

"Multi-tool active," she said. "Track vessel's warp trail."

Every ship at high warp caused a ripple through SlipSpace that could be detected from several lightyears away. The clear visor of her helmet suddenly lit up with an image of the solar system.

A pair of blue dots represented its twin suns, a green dot in the lower left quadrant marked her position. A red dot was slowly moving toward the white circle that marked the solar system's boundary.

The thing about tracking vessels at warp was you could tell *something* was coming your way, but you had no idea what it was. The size of its warp trail would allow you to estimate whether it was a shuttle or a battle cruiser, but that was as good as it got. So, did she activate her distress beacon?

She would have to wait until the Overseers were at least a few lightyears away. At that point, her signal might look like background noise. Multi-tools weren't very powerful transmitters, not like SlipGates. Any ship in the solar system would find her, but beyond that, they would *really* have to be looking.

Of course, that didn't mean there weren't *other* ships waiting around for her to do just that. The Overseers might have left a scout behind. That was the rub. Spotting ships at FTL speeds was easy; spotting ships that were just sitting quietly in the darkness was much more difficult, and the Overseers had clearly been able to hide from her shuttle's instruments. What to do?

Her suit beeped.

New sensor data flashed across the visor; someone was trying to ping her. The ID code listed the caller as "Shuttle Larosa." Her shuttle was still out there! The Overseers hadn't destroyed it; they had merely jammed her transmission. But why-

Of course.

A destroyed shuttle meant that someone had attacked her, and that would lead to an investigation. An empty shuttle meant she had died when the derelict ship exploded. No loose ends.

Jena felt a grin bloom, squeezing her eyes shut. She laughed so hard she almost wheezed. "Execute recovery protocol," she ordered. "Broadcast my location using only standard radio frequencies."

The shuttle was close enough that it wouldn't need FTL communication to locate her. It would hone in on her position, and she would be able to get onboard through the roof hatch. She was going home.

THROUGH THE WINDOW in her small apartment, Jena saw the starry sky above the city of Cairan, tall buildings reaching up toward the heavens with lights in their windows. It was a pretty night, the breeze cool.

"So, you're saying that pirates are responsible for those stasis pods?" Nate Calarin stood in her living room with arms folded. Her bond with her symbiont allowed her to perceive him without having to look. "That pirates destroyed the ship to prevent us from finding evidence of their crimes?"

Chewing on her lower lip, Jena let her head hang. She felt a sudden burst of heat in her cheeks. "They attacked me in the cargo bay," she said. "I guess they figured that they had me outnumbered."

She turned.

A hardwood floor stretched from the mat on which she stood to the pale green wall on the other side of the room, and

Nate stood in the middle, next to her couch. "Pirates seldom challenge Keepers."

Jena frowned, looking down at the floor. She felt strands of dishevelled hair fall over her face. "That's true," she said, nodding. "But like I said, I think they were hoping to kill me before I reported back."

"And after all that," he began. "They just destroyed the ship?"

Jena kept her face smooth as she looked up at him, blinking to feign confusion. "Do I look like a criminal psychologist?" she asked. "Who knows why they do what they do? Maybe they felt the ship would lead us back to them."

Nate grimaced, a rosy hue in his cheeks. He bowed his head, then scrubbed a hand across his brow. "You've left me in a predicament, Jena," he said. "I'm supposed to make a report detailing how pirates destroyed a ship with twelve innocent people onboard."

"Like I said," she growled. "They fought me down to the bowels of the ship, then triggered the auto-destruct. At that point, I could either try to get to the main shuttle bay – which was on the *other* side of the ship – or slip out through an airlock. Either way, I had no time to get *twelve* stasis pods onto a shuttle."

"I see," he mumbled. "And they didn't attack your shuttle?"

"With what weapons?" She spun around, facing the window again. Lying made her belly hurt, but this was necessary. "They had a malfunctioning military vessel and an old cargo hauler. Come on, Nate. Use your brain."

That was harsher than it needed to be.

He turned around, putting his back to her, and marched to the front door. He waited there a moment. "I'm sorry, Jena," he said at last. "I don't mean to berate you. I'm sure it was a harrowing experience."

Jena shut her eyes, a single tear rolling over her cheek.

Damn it but she despised lying! "It's fine," she replied in a rasp. "I just want to slip into the bath tub and forget that today ever happened."

"We'll be patrolling the sector more vigorously."

Jena nodded.

After that, he left. Her heart sank at the thought of misleading him, but she had no other choice. Nate Calarin was a good man, but if she claimed that she'd seen Overseers and fought some of their engineered abominations, he would demand proof. That would lead to an investigation.

She wasn't sure how actively the Overseers monitored human behaviour, but if they could engineer the perfect lure for a Justice Keeper and then set up a trap like that one, it was a good bet they knew a good bit of what went on down here. It wouldn't be long before they figured out that Jena Morane had indeed survived.

The only thing that sheltered her from their wrath was that her sudden death would be conspicuous. Right now, they had incentive to leave her alone, but if she started talking about what had really happened, that might change.

She felt it again – the sensation of being watched. Was it merely in her head, or was there something lurking in her apartment? She needed people she could trust. Deep down, she was still a Justice Keeper.

Justice Keepers did not cower in fear.

Her refusal to carelessly share the details of her experience did not mean she was unwilling to fight back. No one took innocent people and turned them into monsters. Not on her watch. Not in her galaxy. When you got right down to it, just about anything could be killed if you studied it long enough. But she wasn't going to get anything done out here on some backwater colony.

It was time to put in for a transfer, and she knew exactly where she was going to go. The patch on the dead man's uniform had tickled her memory throughout the entire flight back. Checking the computer records had confirmed her suspicions.

That man was from Earth.

Which meant that was the best place to start digging. Worry gnawed at the pit of her stomach. Jena was not stupid. She knew that if she started poking around, sooner or later she would end up pissing off something with a lot of firepower. She could live with that. Better that than a life spent cowering from the unknown. The days ahead would be full of complications and uncertainty, but she was absolutely sure of one thing.

They would be watching her.

ABOUT THE AUTHOR

I wrote this short story while recovering from eye surgery. Problems with my vision are still troubling me today (Feb 2015). So, if you liked this story, please spread the word. The best way you can support this series and ensure that more Justice Keeper novels get published is to create a buzz.

Thank you kindly for your support.

Rich Penney.

Dear reader,

We hope you enjoyed reading *Dark Designs*. Please take a moment to leave a review, even if it's a short one. Your opinion is important to us.

Discover more books by R.S. Penney at https://www.nextchapter.pub/authors/ontario-author-rs-penney

Want to know when one of our books is free or discounted? Join the newsletter at http://eepurl.com/bqqB3H

Best regards,

R.S. Penney and the Next Chapter Team

Dark Designs
ISBN: 978-4-86752-711-5

Published by
Next Chapter
1-60-20 Minami-Otsuka
170-0005 Toshima-Ku, Tokyo
+818035793528

7th August 2021

Lightning Source UK Ltd.
Milton Keynes UK
UKHW010622180821
389030UK00001B/177